PUFFIN BOOKS

The Puffin Book of
Stories for
Six-Year-Olds

Wendy Cooling was educated in Norwich and, after a short time in the Civil Service, spent time travelling the world. On her return to England she trained as a teacher, went on to teach English in London comprehensive schools for many years and was for a time seconded as an advisor on libraries and book-related work in schools. She left teaching to work on the promotion of books and reading as Head of the Children's Book Foundation (now Booktrust), and later founded Bookstart, the national programme that helps to bring books to young readers. She continues to work with the programme as a consultant, as well as working as a freelance book consultant and reviewer.

D0096111

Other books edited by Wendy Cooling

THE PUFFIN BOOK OF STORIES FOR
FIVE-YEAR-OLDS

THE PUFFIN BOOK OF STORIES FOR
SEVEN-YEAR-OLDS

THE PUFFIN BOOK OF STORIES FOR
EIGHT-YEAR-OLDS

THE PUFFIN BOOK OF CHRISTMAS STORIES

D IS FOR DAHL

The Puffin Book of
Stories for

Six-Year-Olds

Edited by Wendy Cooling

Illustrated by Steve Cox

PUFFIN

PUFFIN BOOKS

Published by the Penguin Group
Penguin Books Ltd, 80 Strand, London WC2R 0RL, England
Penguin Group (USA) Inc., 375 Hudson Street, New York, New York 10014, USA
Penguin Group (Canada), 90 Eglinton Avenue East, Suite 700, Toronto, Ontario, Canada M4P 2Y3
(a division of Pearson Penguin Canada Inc.)
Penguin Ireland, 25 St Stephen's Green, Dublin 2, Ireland (a division of Penguin Books Ltd)
Penguin Group (Australia), 250 Camberwell Road, Camberwell, Victoria 3124, Australia
(a division of Pearson Australia Group Pty Ltd)
Penguin Books India Pvt Ltd, 11 Community Centre, Panchsheel Park, New Delhi – 110 017, India
Penguin Group (NZ), 67 Apollo Drive, Mairangi Bay, Auckland 1310, New Zealand
(a division of Pearson New Zealand Ltd)
Penguin Books (South Africa) (Pty) Ltd, 24 Sturdee Avenue, Rosebank, Johannesburg 2196, South Africa

Penguin Books Ltd, Registered Offices: 80 Strand, London WC2R 0RL, England

penguin.com

First published 1996
043

The Acknowledgements on pages 131–2 constitute an extension of this copyright page

Set in Monophoto Ehrhardt
Made and printed in England by Clays Ltd, St Ives plc

British Library Cataloguing in Publication Data
A CIP catalogue record for this book is available from the British Library

ISBN: 978-0-140-37459-9

www.greenpenguin.co.uk

Contents

Introduction   vii

The Martian and the Supermarket
    Penelope Lively   1
Kind Polly and the Wolf in Danger
    Catherine Storr   19
The Hodja and the Saucepan
    Anon.   32
The Thrush Girl   *Godfried Bomans*   34
Ranjit and the Tiger   *Paddy Kinsale*   42
Anna-Magdalena's Dark Secret
    Kay Kinnear   50
The Leaning Silver Birch
    James Riordan   62
Making Pancakes When My Mother
    was Out   *Paddy Kinsale*   64
The Pearl Tree   *Ira Saxena*   70

Careless Conrad   *M. Joyce Davies*   81

How Trouble Made the Monkey Eat
    Pepper   *Grace Hallworth*   99

The Tortoises' Picnic   *Katherine
    Briggs*   103

In the Beginning and Pandora's Box
    Geraldine McCaughrean   106

The Crooked Little Finger
    Philippa Pearce   116

Acknowledgements   131

Introduction

By six, children are well settled in school and are reading, beginning to read, or certainly developing the word and letter recognition and sound associations that take them well along the road to reading. Six-year-olds are of course all different in so many ways, not least in the stages they've reached in their reading development. What they all have in common is that enjoyment of sharing books with a parent, a caring adult or a sibling. They will all be joining in the reading more and more as they will by now know how books work, will recognize words and initial letters, remember stories so well that they almost seem to be reading them and, certainly, six-year-olds will be asking more and more questions.

I hope the stories in this collection are as varied as the many six-year-olds who will read them. They are stories for sharing, for although some children will be ready to read ones like 'Careless Conrad' and 'The Tortoises' Picnic' for themselves, most six-year-olds will need to be introduced to the more difficult ones. For instance, 'In the Beginning and Pandora's Box' will probably be your child's first encounter with Greek myths; you will need to discuss some of the quite complicated ideas it deals with. It's the time to excite young minds, to talk about myths, legends and folk tales – and the time for telling stories. Stories are so important as in storytelling nothing comes between the storyteller and the child. Tales like 'Making Pancakes When Mother was Out' will make you remember your own childhood adventures and family memories – the more you talk about them, the better they get. Your memories will help you to introduce stories from other oral traditions such as 'How Trouble Made the Monkey Eat Pepper'.

INTRODUCTION

So, this is a collection of stories that will touch the imagination and encourage questions. Some are from other lands, some set against everyday backgrounds and some are fantastical. They're about ordinary people, gods, kings, animals, Martians and sea-captains – enjoy them all!

Wendy Cooling

The Martian and the Supermarket

PENELOPE LIVELY

It was the middle of the night when the rocket landed in the supermarket car-park. The engine had failed. The hatch opened and the Martian peered out. A Martian, I should tell you, is about three feet high and has webbed feet, green skin and eyes on the ends of horns like a snail. This one, who was three hundred and twenty-seven years old, wore a red jersey.

He said, "Bother!" He had only passed his driving test the week before and was always losing his way. He was an extremely

1

nervous person, and felt the cold badly. He shivered. A car hooted and he scuttled behind a rubbish bin. Everything looked very strange and frightening.

It began to rain. He wrapped himself in a newspaper, but the rain soon came through that. And then he saw that a sliding door into the back of the supermarket had been left a little bit open, just enough for him to wriggle through.

It was warmer inside, but just as frightening. There were large glass cases that hummed to themselves, and slippery floors, and piles and piles of brightly coloured tins and boxes. He couldn't imagine what it was all for. He curled up between two of the humming cases and went to sleep.

He woke up to find everything brightly lit. He could hear people talking and walking about. He tucked himself as far out of sight as possible. Feet passed him, and silver things on wheels. Once, one with a baby in it stopped just by him. The baby leaned out and saw him and began to cry.

"Ssh . . ." whispered the Martian. The

baby continued to shriek until its mother moved the pram on.

The Martian couldn't think what he should do. He was hungry and he wanted to go home and the bright lights and loud noises in this place made him jump. He began to cry; tears trickled down his horns. He sniffed, loudly.

It was at this moment that a girl called Judy stopped right beside him. Her mother was hunting for fish fingers in the freezer and Judy was pushing the trolley and also wishing she could go home; she hated shopping. She heard a peculiar fizzing noise come from the gap between the fish-fingers freezer and the one beside it, and looked in.

Plenty of people, looking between two freezers in a supermarket and seeing a thing there like a three-foot green snail with a red jersey on would have screamed. Or fainted. I think I would have. Not so Judy. She bent down for a closer look.

"Please don't tell anyone," said the Martian. "They might be unkind to me."

"Are you a boy or a girl?" asked Judy.

3

"I'm not sure. Does it matter?"

"Sometimes," said Judy, after a moment's thought. "It depends how you're feeling." She studied the Martian with care. "I think you're a boy. It's something about your eyes. Never mind. Some boys I quite like. How did you get here?"

"My rocket went wrong and I'd lost the map. Do you think you could help me get away?"

Judy thought about this. "I would if I could."

"I don't want to stay here," – the Martian's voice shook – "All these people make me nervous and the noise gives me a headache."

Judy looked round. Her mother had met a friend and was busy chatting. "Tell you what," she said. "Come home with us and I'll think of something."

"Will it be all right?" said the Martian doubtfully.

"I don't know," said Judy. "But let's try it anyway and see. Quick – get into the box." Her mother had put a cardboard box into the trolley, ready to stack the

4

shopping in. Judy looked round again – her mother was still chatting – grabbed the Martian, bundled him into the box and shut the flaps.

"I'm a bit squashed," said the Martian in a muffled voice. At that moment Judy's mother finished her chat and they were off to the meat counter.

When they got to the check-out Judy quickly grabbed another box and piled the shopping into that. Her mother, when she had found the right money and paid the girl at the till, was surprised they had enough to fill two boxes.

"It's always more than you think," said Judy cheerfully. She picked up the box with the Martian in it and carried it to the car.

At home, it was an easy matter to let him out while her mother was opening the door and whisk him round into the garage and behind the lawn-mower. The cat, who had been sleeping there on an old sack, gave one look and fled, howling. It wasn't seen again for two days.

"Make yourself at home," said Judy.

"I'll bring you some lunch when I can. Sorry I can't ask you into the house, but you know what mothers are . . ."

The Martian said he quite understood – he had one himself. "I don't want to be a nuisance," he added humbly.

She brought him beefburgers for lunch, which he liked, and sponge-cake for tea, which he didn't, though he was too polite to say so. She also brought him some books in case he was bored, and before Judy's bedtime they played cards for a bit. The Martian was quite good at Snap, and even managed to win a couple of times. His horns went slightly pink when he was excited.

It is not the easiest thing in the world to keep a visitor of this kind in your garage without anyone else in the family knowing about it. Judy told the Martian to hide behind a pile of deck-chairs when either her mother or her father came.

She and the Martian soon became fond of each other.

"If a person's nice," said Judy, "it really

6

doesn't matter what they look like." Which was perhaps not the most tactful thing in the world to say, though she meant well.

"Thank you," said the Martian. "That's just what I've always felt myself." Truth to tell, he thought Judy was pretty odd-looking.

Judy was worried that he might be getting bored. It didn't seem any way to treat a visitor – hiding behind a lawn-mower in the garage all day.

"Tell you what," she said, "my great-aunt's coming over this evening while Mum and Dad are out. You could come into the house and watch telly. She's so shortsighted she'd never notice you aren't one of my ordinary friends."

The Martian was doubtful. "Are great-aunts fierce?"

"Not this one," said Judy.

So, that evening, Judy and the Martian sat on the sofa and watched telly while Great-Aunt Nora sat in the armchair and interrupted. She asked the Martian how old he was and what class he was in at school and where he went for his holidays last year.

"Jupiter," said the Martian shyly.

Judy gave him a nudge. "He means Cornwall, Auntie."

"That's nice," said Aunt Nora. She changed her reading-glasses for her other glasses and peered over at the Martian. "Have you been ill, dear? You're not a very good colour, are you? I think your mother ought to be giving you a tonic."

"He's had chicken-pox," said Judy.

"Chicken-pox was spots when I was young," said Aunt Nora, "not anything like he's got."

"There are horrible new kinds of chicken-pox now," said Judy. Aunt Nora tutted and moved her chair a little further away.

The Martian quite enjoyed watching telly. He said he thought they used to have something like that where he came from back in the old days.

At nine o'clock, well before Judy's parents came back, the Martian slipped out to the garage again. Aunt Nora reported to Judy's mum that Judy's friend was a nice child, but a bit unhealthy-looking.

"Who was it?" asked Judy's mum. "Susie? Ben?"

"Someone new I've got to know," said Judy. Which was perfectly true. No more questions were asked, luckily.

On another day Judy managed to stay at home while her mother went to visit a friend. It was a sunny day and was a chance to get the Martian out in the garden for some fresh air. She bought them both an ice lolly from the corner shop and they settled down at the end of the lawn for a game of Snap. At which point, of course, the next-door neighbour, Mrs Potter, came out to hang up her washing and looked over the fence.

Judy hissed at the Martian to keep absolutely still. She went over to the fence and said good morning to Mrs Potter, specially politely.

Mrs Potter stared over the top of Judy's head. "My goodness, Judy, whatever is that? Sitting on the grass over there . . ."

"It's a garden gnome," said Judy promptly.

"Well!" said Mrs Potter. "I can't say I like the look of it much."

"Nor does Mum," said Judy. "She's sending it back. Don't say anything about it. She's a bit upset."

Mrs Potter nodded understandingly.

Judy, you will have realized, was someone who was pretty quick off the mark. Never at a loss. Even so, it was clear that things could not go on like this for ever. And the Martian was getting more and more homesick. Sometimes he sat behind the lawn-mower quietly sniffing for hours on end. Judy felt really sorry for him.

She told the Martian that she would go to the supermarket with her mother the next day and see if his rocket was still in the car-park.

The Martian brightened up. Then he said gloomily, "But even if it was, how would I get back to it?"

"I'll think of something," said Judy. "Don't worry."

But there was absolutely no sign of the rocket in the supermarket car-park. Judy had a good look round while her mother was inside. Come to think of it, a small red rocket wasn't really the sort of thing that would have been left to lie around for several days. The question was – who had taken it and what had they done with it? She went into the supermarket to find her mother and help with the shopping.

When they got to the check-out her mother said, "Well! I see they've got something to amuse the toddlers now."

There, just by the exit, was the red rocket, mounted on a stand, sparkling with yellow lights and with a notice beside it saying TEN PENCE A RIDE. A mother put ten pence in the slot, popped her baby in the rocket and the rocket jiggled about and flashed its lights. The baby beamed out through the plastic hatch.

Judy stared. She hoped it wouldn't take off. But no – after a few minutes the rocket stopped jiggling, the mother lifted the baby out and put him in a pushchair.

As soon as she got home she rushed out to the garage to tell the Martian. He looked alarmed.

"This is terrible! If they haven't got it properly fixed it could take off."

"They think it's just a toy," said Judy.

The Martian got very distressed. "It's this year's model. Goes faster than sound if you want it to, not that I've ever dared. Something dreadful could happen if they keep it there."

Judy thought of babies whizzing out of the supermarket faster than sound. She nodded. Quite true – you could upset a person for life, having that sort of thing happen to them at that age.

"What we have got to do," she said, "is get *you* into it."

It would not be easy to get him back to the supermarket without Judy's mother noticing. Mothers, as you no doubt know, have a way of apparently paying no attention and then suddenly pouncing on anything unusual. But eventually they worked out a plan.

The next time Judy's mother was getting ready to go shopping Judy popped into the garage ahead of her, helped the Martian climb into the back seat of the car and bundled him up in her anorak.

When they got to the supermarket she tucked the whole bundle of anorak and Martian under her arm and carried it in after her mother. She was puffing and blowing with the weight. Her mother said, "Put your coat on – no need to carry it around like that."

"I'd be too hot," said Judy. One of the Martian's webbed feet was poking out. She tucked a sleeve round it.

"Suit yourself," said her mother.

The shopping seemed to take for ever that morning. First her mother forgot the eggs and had to go all the way back to the start to collect them. Then she met a friend. Then she couldn't decide what to have for supper. Judy staggered along behind. The Martian seemed heavier and heavier.

"Judy," said her mother. "Just run back and pick up another loaf, will you?"

Judy sighed. She walked back down the aisle. A woman with a very full trolley, not looking where she was going, came round a corner smack into her.

"Oops!" said the woman. "Sorry, love!"

Judy lurched into a mountain of corn-flake packets and dropped the anorak. The Martian rolled out and dived, quick as a flash, behind a display of dustpans.

"Gracious!" exclaimed the woman. "Was that your dog? You're not allowed to bring dogs in here, you know."

Judy could see the Martian cowering behind the dustpans.

Several people had stopped to see what the fuss was about. Judy did some quick thinking. She took a deep breath and burst into tears.

"Ah . . ." said someone. "What's the matter, dear?"

"I've lost my mum," wailed Judy.

"Poor little soul," said another woman. "There . . . we'll soon find her."

Judy was the centre of attention. The Martian kept as still as still. Judy watched him out of the corner of one eye and went on crying with the other.

Her mother appeared round a corner. "Where have you been, for goodness' sake, Judy? And whatever's the matter?"

About five kind, motherly ladies were patting Judy and promising to look after her. Judy wriggled free and flung herself at her mother. Everyone beamed, except Judy's mother, who knew Judy and didn't believe a word of it. She marched off towards the checkout with one hand firmly on Judy's shoulder.

As soon as they were standing in the line to pay, Judy cried, "Help . . . forgot my anorak . . . sorry . . ." and dashed back to the dustpan display. She scooped the Martian up in the anorak and came rushing back.

"Sorry about all this," she whispered. "Just hang on a bit longer. Soon get everything sorted out."

There was a long line at the checkout. Judy could see the rocket flashing and jiggling. A baby was having a ride on it.

Judy slipped away from her mother and stood near them. Her mother was busy taking her shopping out of the trolley for the checkout lady. She looked up and said, "Judy! Don't go wandering off!"

"Just watching the rocket, Mum," said Judy.

The Martian poked one horn out from under the anorak and said, "I'm ever so nervous."

"So am I," said Judy. "The thing is, how're we going to get it off that stand they've put it on?"

The Martian peered a little further. "There are two screws. You'll have to undo them. Do you think you can?"

"I s'pect so," said Judy.

The rocket stopped jiggling. The mother lifted her baby out. Judy stepped forward and popped the Martian into the rocket, still wrapped up in the anorak.

"Giving your little brother a turn?" said the baby's mother.

"That's right," said Judy. "He's mad about space travel." She bent down.

"I shouldn't touch those screws, dear," said the woman.

"I'm just checking that it's safe," said Judy sternly.

Luckily the baby, who had caught sight of the Martian's horns, was now howling. Its mother turned away.

"I've done them," hissed Judy. "Are you ready?"

"All systems go," said the Martian. "That's what you're supposed to say, isn't it?"

"I think so," said Judy. She whipped her anorak off him and closed the hatch. "Well . . . Bye then. It's been ever so nice having you."

"Thank *you*," said the Martian. "I'll send you a postcard when I get back. Bye . . ."

Judy stepped aside and put ten pence in the slot. The rocket's lights flashed. It began to jiggle around and . . .

. . . Well, they are still talking about it in the town where Judy lives. At least those who saw it happen are. Those who didn't, say it was all imagination. But there are at least twenty people who saw a small red rocket go zooming three times round the supermarket and then out of the doors.

The local paper had a headline that said MYSTERY BABY TAKES OFF! And of course nobody ever reported a missing child. So after a while people lost interest, though the supermarket manager is still looking for that toy rocket he found in the car park. It had been very useful for amusing the toddlers.

And after a couple of weeks Judy got a postcard of some very peculiar mountains, with stamps on the other side the like of which no one had ever seen.

Kind Polly and the Wolf in Danger

CATHERINE STORR

This story is different from all the other stories about Polly and the wolf, because it doesn't start with the wolf planning how he can have Polly to eat.

One day, Polly went out to do some shopping for her mother in the village. She had bought a cauliflower and some potatoes at the vegetable shop, and a pound of sugar and half a pound of biscuits at the grocer's, and she was thinking of going home again, when she heard a loud noise coming from a side street. She ran to the corner and looked along the street and saw a crowd of people all very angry about something. The people were shouting and someone was howling. Polly thought that she knew that howl, and she hurried up the street.

As she got nearer the crowd, she could hear more distinctly what the people were saying.

"Ought not to be allowed!"

"Would worry the sheep!"

"Cause a dog fight!"

"Steal a hen!"

"These beasts are dangerous. Should be behind bars!"

"Might bite a baby!"

"Could easily kill a child!"

"Someone muzzle it!"

"Someone shoot it!"

Polly began to believe that she knew whom the voices were talking about, but she still hadn't managed to get through the crowd to see if she had guessed right. Now she heard other voices saying other things.

"Interesting shape. Don't know if I've

20

ever seen one exactly like that before. A new breed, perhaps?"

"Look it up in the *Gazette*."

"Like to have a look at its bones. Preserve the skeleton in formaldehyde . . ."

"Curious sound it makes. Don't know if I've ever heard a dog howl exactly like that . . ."

Polly pushed through the inner ring of trousers and skirts and saw a wooden tea chest set up on end. Out of the top of the tea chest stuck the head of the wolf, and over his head, someone had thrown a net, which was held down by the edges of the chest. The wolf was in a bad way. His fur was draggled, he was trembling and he was looking this way and that with huge, terrified eyes.

"It'd make a splendid exhibit for the local museum. Stuffed, of course," a large man in a tweed jacket was saying. Polly saw a glimmer of hope cross the wolf's face, and she realized that he was thinking of being stuffed as an agreeable sensation after a large meal. But the hope disappeared the next moment, as a woman

21

added, "You have to be careful how you kill an animal you want to stuff. A bullet through the heart is fine, but whoever shoots must know how to be accurate."

"I'm against killing. This animal should be in a zoo," another woman said.

"Doesn't look in very good shape to me. Death might be a mercy," a man said.

"Shouldn't be shot, though. Call in the local vet."

"Spoilsport! Why not have a chase? We could get the hounds. Creature would enjoy a good run for its money," said another voice.

"Cruel! I object! No blood sports here!" said someone else.

"In any case its body should be preserved for expert examination."

"Call the police!"

"Send for the Master of the Hunt!"

"Fetch my gun!"

The voices grew louder and more quarrelsome. Everyone seemed to be shouting at everyone else. Polly managed to edge closer. "Wolf!" she said.

The wolf turned his miserable eyes towards her.

"You here?" he said.

"What happened? Why are they all so angry? What did you do?"

"I didn't do anything," the wolf said, sullenly.

"I don't believe that. Tell me the truth."

"I didn't do anything out of the ordinary. I've seen plenty of people do it."

"Go on."

"I've often seen people go round sniffing at other people's babies."

"Sniffing at them?" Polly asked, surprised.

"Bending right over their prams, with their noses in the children's faces. And you can hear them smacking their lips."

"Probably kissing them."

"Nonsense! Sniffing to see if they're ready to eat. Smacking their lips when they know what a good meal they're going to have."

"Is that what you did?" Polly asked.

"Only one or two. The first was a

scrawny little thing, not worth its salt. The second wasn't any good, either. It hit me. I did not hit back. Naturally I didn't want a struggle."

"And then?"

"Then I saw exactly what I needed. Small, plump, juicy-looking. Not unlike you, a few years ago. I was just unwrapping it, to make sure it was perfectly fresh, when this woman came dashing out of the shop and started screeching and calling me all sorts of names, and then a couple of men came up and got hold of my legs, and they held my jaws so that I couldn't speak, and they pushed me into this revolting box and covered me with a net."

"Oh Wolf! What did you expect? Had you forgotten that people don't eat babies?"

"I can't think why not. There seems to be a very good supply," the wolf said.

"Would you eat wolf cubs?"

"Certainly. If I was hungry."

"Well, most people don't eat babies. So when they saw you sniffing into prams, they realized that you weren't a human. They knew you were a wolf."

24

"No, they don't. They don't know what I am. Didn't you hear what they said? They think I'm very unusual," wolf said, with a little pride.

"Don't be too pleased about that. It's because you're so unusual that they want to dissect you."

"What's dissect?" the wolf asked.

"Cut you up to find out how you work."

"Cut me up alive!" the wolf cried.

"Not alive. Dead."

"Cut me up, dead?"

"Or shoot you and stuff you. Not with food. With cotton wool, or whatever you stuff dead creatures with," Polly explained.

The wolf shuddered.

"Or they might want to hunt you. With dogs."

"What am I going to do?" the wolf said, and at his howl, several people in the crowd turned round to see what was happening.

"Don't stand so close, little girl. That animal is dangerous," a man in spectacles said.

25

"I've met him before," Polly said.

"Then you know that he is a threat to our community," Spectacles said.

Polly thought quickly. "I'll tell you what I do know. He's a very strange animal. There's never been anything quite like him here before." (That's true enough, she said to herself.) "In fact he's Unique."

"I am NOT," she heard the wolf mutter behind the net, but she took no notice and went on.

"You know what a fuss everyone makes about not letting rare kinds of plants and animals disappear. I can tell you, if you hurt this animal, there's going to be a terrible fuss. You'll get blamed by everyone important. The Queen will be angry, and the Prime Minister will be furious, and I wouldn't wonder if the whole village didn't get punished."

There were murmurs among the crowd. They were obviously impressed. She heard, "Seems to know what she's talking about." "Don't want the place to get a bad name." "Remember what the Green Party said on television the other night, about preserving the balance of Nature."

26

"I expect one of the television stars would tell everyone what a terrible thing had happened here," Polly said, reminded of the power of TV.

"She's right. We don't want to be held up to scorn as vandals," the tweedy man said.

"Animal Rights," said a thin woman who hadn't spoken before.

"I still think it should be put behind bars. In a zoo," said a fat man.

"Polly! I won't go into a zoo," the wolf said in an undertone.

"Can't I have it to keep in my room?" a small boy asked his mum, who said, "Sorry, sweetie, I don't think Dad would like it."

"That wouldn't be too bad," the wolf said, looking over the small boy hungrily.

"He shouldn't be in a zoo. He should be allowed to roam free," Polly said.

"Not around our village!" someone said quickly.

"Where he belongs. In forests, or on hills. Wherever he came from," the thin woman said.

"Where did you come from, Wolf?"

27

Polly asked, wondering why she had never asked this question before.

"Can't remember. I didn't come out of a box, I do know that."

"In fact, he's almost certainly one of an endangered species," Polly said.

"I don't! I wouldn't, anyway, if you let me go!" the wolf cried.

"Wouldn't what?" Polly asked.

"Make dangerous speeches. It's not the sort of thing I do."

"I didn't say speeches, I said . . . what that means is that you're very special and we ought to take great care nothing terrible happens to you."

"Now that makes sense . . . Why don't all the other . . ." the wolf began, but he was interrupted by the man in spectacles, who had raised his hand and said, "Ahem! Ahem! It seems to me that we should take a vote on the question of what to do with this . . . this . . . unusual animal. I for one am not prepared to take the responsibility of advising its destruction . . ."

"What's that?" the wolf whispered to Polly.

28

"Killing you," Polly whispered back.

". . . by whatever means. The choice therefore lies between sending it to one of the many zoological institutions in this country, or, as my friend here has suggested, letting it go free to its natural habitat . . ."

"Natural what?" the wolf wanted to know.

"Where you live, Wolf."

". . . wherever that may be. Could we have a show of hands, please? Those wishing the animal to go to a zoo put up their hands."

He counted. "Four . . . six . . . Are you holding up your hand, Madam, or adjusting a hatpin? . . . Seven . . ."

"Wolf! If I loosened the net here, could you creep out?" Polly whispered. She had discovered that she could pull the edge of the net a little away from the bottom of the tea chest.

"If I make myself very thin."

"And if I do, will you promise . . . ?" But Spectacles had now finished the first count and there were too many people

29

looking round. Polly waited till she heard the second counting begin. Then she finished the sentence. "Will you promise not to try to catch me to eat ever again?"

"Of course. I promise. Now let me out," the Wolf said, far too quickly.

"You didn't mean that. Think about it."

The wolf thought. "You mean really, truly, never?"

"Really, truly, never."

"But it's been fun! Hasn't it?"

"Sometimes. Frightening, too."

"Being frightened is fun. And anyway, you're so clever, Polly. You've always managed to escape up till now."

"You've never said I was clever before," Polly said.

"I didn't realize how clever you are till I heard you say that about dangerous speeches," the wolf said.

Polly was pleased. She began to say, "Well, just promise . . ." But the sentence never got said, for at that moment the wolf, seeing that she wasn't thinking about holding the net as tightly as before, pushed his head up and pulled it out of her hands. There was a bump, a crash, and a moment later, the wolf was out of the tea chest, free of the net, and was streaking down the High Street, terrifying passers-by and only just avoiding cars and bicycles.

Luckily no one blamed Polly. "But I wonder what he thinks his natural habitat is? I'm sure it's not forests or hills, it's much more likely to be this village where he knows his way around," she thought and wondered if she would ever see him again. Probably. He wasn't likely to give up now that on this occasion it had been the wolf who had flattered and fooled her. Clever Polly had for once met a not so stupid wolf.

The Hodja and the Saucepan

(ANON.)

One day the Hodja borrowed a large saucepan from his neighbour. When he took it back there was a small saucepan inside.

"What's this?" asked his neighbour, pointing to the small saucepan.

"You have a very remarkable saucepan," said the Hodja. "That's a baby. Your saucepan had a baby the other day."

The neighbour thanked the Hodja and took the pans off to his kitchen.

A few days later the Hodja again came to borrow the large saucepan.

"Of course," said the neighbour, with a wide smile. "Whenever you like."

When several weeks had passed and the Hodja still had not returned the saucepan his neighbour went round to see him.

"Your saucepan?" said the Hodja when the owner asked for it. "Didn't I tell you? It died."

"Died!" shouted his neighbour. "Died! How can a saucepan die?"

"It was a very remarkable saucepan," said the Hodja. "First it had a baby, then it died."

The Thrush Girl

GODFRIED BOMANS

Once upon a time there was a little girl who longed to be able to understand animals. She went to her old grandmother and said: "Oh, grandmother, I would so love to understand the animals. Can you teach me how to do it?"

The grandmother could do a little magic, but not much.

"Oh, my child," she said, "I can only understand the thrushes, and that is not worth the trouble."

"It is enough for me," replied the little girl. "Please teach me."

So the grandmother taught the little girl to understand the thrushes. It was much easier than she had thought. She had only to be kind to the birds and throw them a few crumbs from time to time.

And when she had learned, she walked through the woods listening to the thrushes. Her grandmother was right. They had not much to say. But the little girl was right, too, because it was enough for her. And she went to her father and said: "Father, bring in the hay, for it will rain tomorrow."

The father believed the child. He brought in the hay and by evening it was stacked in the barn. The next morning it began to rain. All the hay in the district was soaked and only his was dry. The father was glad he had listened to his child, but all the other farmers were angry. They were not pleased about the hay that had been saved; they thought only of their own loss. "That girl is no good," they said, "she will go to the bad."

But the little girl said nothing. She went back to her grandmother and said: "Now I would like to understand the moles as well."

"Oh, my child," replied the grandmother, "what a lot you want. Just be good to the animals, then you will understand them after a time."

It was three months before the little girl could understand the moles, too. And one day she said to her father: "Bury the potatoes deep in the ground, for tomorrow it will freeze."

And sure enough, next day it froze. The father had buried his potatoes deep in the ground and they were undamaged. All the other farmers moaned and groaned, for they had not a single good potato left. He had warned them all, but they had not listened to him. They thought the little girl was bewitched. The little girl said nothing. Now she wanted to understand the language of the bees, too. Her grandmother could not help her, for she herself could not understand the bees.

"You know more than I now," she said. "You must learn to talk with bees in your own way."

So the little girl was very kind to the bees. She no longer ate honey, but left what there was in the hives. And after a little while she could understand exactly what the bees were saying to each other. And one day she went to her mother and said: "Prop up the fruit trees in the orchard and lock the windows tight, for there will be a great storm tonight."

And that very evening a mighty wind rose up and devastated all the houses. The trees bowed and broke and there was great distress in the land. Only the orchard in which the little girl lived stood upright and not a tree was harmed. Other people grew so angry that they said: "The child is bewitched! We will burn her!"

The people came running from every side with dry branches to build a great fire. The little girl stood on top of the pile of branches and called in a loud voice: "Thrushes, thrushes, help me now!"

The people could not understand what she was saying, for it was in bird language, but the thrushes understood her perfectly. And in their thousands they flew down and each plucked a twig from the fire. The little girl was soon standing on the grass and there was no more firewood to be seen. She ran happily home and cried: "Father, mother, the birds have set me free!"

Oh, how happy they were! But their joy did not last long, for the king's soldiers knocked at the door.

"Open!" they cried. "We have come to fetch the girl!"

She was taken to the market-place and there stood a man with a great gleaming axe.

"Your head must come off," he said. "Kneel down and stretch out your neck."

The little girl did as she was told, but as she laid her head on the block she cried in a loud voice: "Bees, bees, help me now!"

The executioner did not understand her, for she spoke in bee language. But the bees understood her perfectly. And just as the executioner raised his axe, there came a loud humming and thousands of bees dived at him with their stings ready to strike. The executioner fell to the ground, dead, and the king's soldiers scattered in terror. The little girl ran home at top speed and cried: "Father, mother, here I am! The bees have saved me!"

But now the king himself took a hand. He rang the bell and said: "I have come to fetch your daughter. I cannot kill her. But she shall be shut up in a stone tower."

So the girl was taken to a tower with walls fifteen feet thick. The windows had iron bars and the door was shut with three locks. It was so dark that she could see nothing, but she heard the rats and mice scuttling across the stone floor. The little girl sat on the ground and began to weep bitterly.

"I shall never get out," she said. "Oh, moles, moles, help me now!"

No sooner had she said this than thousands of moles began to tunnel under the tower. The walls began to tilt and topple. The floor burst open and the bars sprang out of the window-frames. And suddenly, crash! The tower fell with a roar that reverberated throughout the country. The king was just having breakfast when he heard it. He put down his knife and fork and said: "The tower has fallen. Did you hear it?"

"Yes, father," said the prince. "Shall I marry her now?"

"I think you should," said the king, "although she is rather small."

And together they stepped into their coach with the four horses and rode at full speed to the house where the little girl lived. She was standing in the garden, scattering crumbs for the birds.

"Will you marry me, later on?" asked the prince.

"No," said the little girl, "I will not. I do not like the people here. I shall go away."

She packed three jam sandwiches in her

basket and added a few blackcurrants. Then she put on her fur-trimmed cloak and went away. And no one ever saw her again.

Ranjit and the Tiger

PADDY KINSALE

Ranjit walked from his village to the edge of the jungle. Then he saw something that made his heart jump. A tiger!

He ran as fast as his legs would carry him. He looked behind and WHAM! Down he fell.

His foot was tangled in the creeper. He looked round but where was the tiger? Why didn't the tiger chase him? He looked hard. The tiger was still there – Ranjit could see him.

Perhaps the tiger was hurt. Perhaps he had his foot caught in a creeper as well.

It took Ranjit a long time but he got his foot loose at last and he ran for all he was worth. Then he slowed down. What about the tiger? What would happen to him? He would starve to death. Or the hunters would come and shoot him.

Ranjit felt bad about the tiger now. He stopped. He turned round. He started to walk back.

The tiger was still there, looking at him. The tiger didn't look very fierce. He looked sad. Ranjit went closer. He knelt down and put out his hand towards the tiger's head. The tiger didn't move. Then Ranjit saw that the tiger's foot was caught in a tangle of creepers. It was bleeding. Ranjit moved his hand closer and the tiger moved his head a little. But he didn't growl, nor did he snarl. He let Ranjit undo the creeper from his foot. It was hard work and took a long time. The foot was bleeding a lot and the tiger began to lick it.

Ranjit stood up and slowly walked away. There was no more he could do. He hoped the tiger wouldn't leap on him when his back was turned.

After a while he looked round. The tiger was following him. He waited. The tiger came up to him. He was limping. The tiger rubbed his nose against Ranjit's side. He was being friendly. Ranjit put out his hand and stroked the tiger's thick golden hair.

"You'd better go back," he said and walked away. But the tiger still followed him.

Ranjit thought about it. If he went home with the tiger everybody would be terrified. Somebody might try to shoot him. So he turned round and went with the tiger back to the jungle.

The tiger quietly padded along at his side. He let Ranjit stroke his head and fondle his ears. He didn't mind. Sometimes he would rub his nose on Ranjit's side. Ranjit was very pleased to have such a great friend. After all, the tiger was king of the animals in this jungle.

After a while Ranjit began to think the tiger was leading him.

Perhaps he's taking me to his lair, thought Ranjit. Well, I might as well go

44

with him, now I've come this far. So on he went.

Ranjit saw many creatures in the jungle, such as the cobra, wild pig, and monkeys chattering away in the trees. They soon scuttled away when they saw he was with the tiger.

Presently they came to a place where there was a huge rock covered all over with creepers and roots from the trees that grew out high above it. Ranjit followed the tiger down a track. It wasn't easy. They scrambled over some rocks and then at last there was the entrance to a cave.

As Ranjit climbed up behind the tiger he saw that there were cubs in the cave. Coming out quickly was a tigress. Ranjit was afraid for he knew that female tigers were very fierce, especially when they had cubs. But when they all saw Ranjit's tiger they were friendly. They came up to Ranjit and rubbed against him. He was very proud. He was probably the only boy in the world to have a family of tigers for his friends.

Ranjit was happy staying with the tigers.

He played with the cubs who kept running into each other and falling over, and he explored the cave which went deep into the mountain and once he had a ride on the tigress's back. He had to hold on very tight because she moved so fast through the forest.

But he couldn't stay there for ever. He had to get back home. His mother would worry about him if he was out after dark.

"Goodbye, tigers," he said. He knew they could not understand him but he felt he had to say something to them. He stroked each one of them in turn and patted their heads which they seemed to like. Then he waved goodbye and set off for home.

But he didn't feel so safe in the jungle as he did when he was with the tiger. There were strange moving shapes of animals. He knew that there were creatures lurking in the dark places of the forest. He hurried on. Sometimes he saw the swift movement of the cobras in the bushes and he ran, cutting his arms on sharp branches. He was beginning to wish he had stayed with the tigers. But now he had to keep on to his village. He knew the way for he was used to the jungle. His father had taken him into it many times when he was hunting. But always his father had a fine gun. Now he was alone with no weapons.

He heard a sound behind him and, turning, he tripped and fell. He was soon on his feet again but when he looked up there in a tree just above him was the long and powerful body of a leopard. It was staring straight at Ranjit and its mouth was curled up in an ugly snarl. Ranjit knew that it was getting ready to leap. If he ran it would soon catch up with him. If he stayed there it would leap out on to him. What could he do? If only he could call his tiger friends.

It was his only chance. He put his hands to his mouth and shouted in a loud voice: "GOODBYE TIGERS." He hoped the tigers would hear him and recognize his voice.

The leopard was surprised by the call

and stopped for a minute. He didn't know what to make of the call.

Ranjit stood his ground and stared at the leopard. The leopard stared at him. The leopard wasn't sure what to do. He crouched ready to spring and with a snarl on his face, but he didn't spring. And then Ranjit heard it.

The sound of the tiger. So his friend had heard him.

The tiger came bounding up, huge and fierce. It leapt up at the leopard who drew back spitting and snarling. The tiger lashed out with his terrible claws. The leopard shrank back and then he turned tail and bounded away into another tree and into the jungle.

Ranjit turned to his friend.

"Thank you, tiger," he said. "I did you a good turn, and now you have done one for me."

He said goodbye to the tiger once more and set out for home. He didn't have far to go now. Before he stepped out of the forest he turned and looked back. The tiger was still standing there in the path staring after him. He waved and hurried on.

When he got back he was very tempted to tell all about the tiger, but he didn't. He thought they would say he was making it up, or more likely they would want to go and hunt the tiger with the big gun.

So Ranjit kept quiet about it and never told a soul.

Only sometimes when he had nothing to do he would wander into the jungle and call to his friends, or perhaps stroll up to their cave.

They never forgot him. And he knew that whatever dangers there were in the jungle, he at least was safe from them when his friends the tigers were about.

Anna-Magdalena's Dark Secret

KAY KINNEAR

Anna-Magdalena was a small person with blue eyes and orange hair. She had a straight fringe that she blew off her forehead whenever she was worried or cross. More often than not, her face wore a determined "I-know-what-I-know" expression.

One of the things that Anna-Magdalena knew was that she loved her big, long name, all of it. But her family simply wouldn't use it. Mum and her stepdad, Gerald, called her Mags. So did Aunty Cath. Her Uncle Henry was even more hopeless. He called her Sausage. Worst of all, though she loved him dearly, was her Uncle Andy. He had orange hair just like hers and he was always calling her by different names. It could be Mags. It could be Maggy-Waggy, even Anna-Banana. It was very discouraging.

Last year, though, Anna-Magdalena had outsmarted her family. When Mum had a new baby, Anna-Magdalena had picked out his name. She chose Luke. It was a name so short that even *her* family couldn't find silly things to do with it. Baby Luke was crawling now and Anna-Magdalena often told him, "I'll teach you to say my name right."

So far, all he could say was, "durdle, durdle, durdle."

Anna-Magdalena never gave up on things easily. She was also quite a brave little girl. She liked the highest slide at the park. She wasn't afraid of water, even though she'd had to try and try before she learned to swim. She wasn't even afraid of spiders now.

But there *was* one thing Anna-

Magdalena was frightened of. She was afraid of the dark. She hadn't told anybody. It was a secret.

In fact, it was such a secret that Anna-Magdalena hadn't known it herself until just this week when she broke the little nightlight on her bedside table. The light gave a friendly glow whenever she woke in the dark.

But two days ago, Anna-Magdalena had bounced into bed with her arms stretched out pretending to be a plane. Her right arm (or rather her right wing) clipped the lamp and sent it flying, and it fell onto the hard wooden floor and broke.

Mum sighed and picked up the broken pieces. Then Anna-Magdalena said her bedtime prayers. She asked God to bless everyone in her family. She said "God bless Mummy and Gerald and Luke. God bless Aunty Cath and Uncle Henry. God bless Uncle Andy. And God bless me."

"And help make you more careful," added Mum.

"And help make me more careful," prayed Anna-Magdalena. Being careful was not one of her strong points.

She snuggled down in her bed and went to sleep before her Uncle Andy could have said "Anna-Banana" five times.

Several hours later, Anna-Magdalena woke up. The room was completely black. There was no friendly glow from her bedside lamp. She didn't know where she was and suddenly she felt afraid. She reached out her hand and it bumped into her teddy, who was called Bear.

She hugged Bear to her chest and slid further down into the bed. She whispered to herself, that in a moment or two, when she and Bear were feeling braver, they would go and ask Mum to turn on the landing light.

A few moments later, and before Bear had enough courage to get out of bed, Anna-Magdalena had fallen asleep again.

In the morning the sun streamed in through the window and Anna-Magdalena's bedroom looked the friendliest place in the world. She dragged Bear out from the very bottom of the bed where he had hidden.

"You were silly last night," Anna-Magdalena said to the furry face and gave him a little shake. And then she forgot all about the darkness of the night.

Until bedtime. After her prayers, Anna-Magdalena said to her mum, "I miss my light."

Mum nodded. "I'll get a new one next time I go shopping. Meanwhile I'll turn on the landing light. It'll shine into your room."

In the middle of the night Anna-Magdalena had a bad dream. In the dream something she couldn't see very well was chasing her. She tried to run, but her legs wouldn't move. She shouted in her sleep and woke up.

The landing light *wasn't* on! The room was totally dark and Anna-Magdalena started to cry. She heard footsteps. The bedroom light came on and Anna-Magdalena was gathered into her mum's arms.

"Mags, I'm so sorry. Without thinking, I switched off the landing light when I went to bed."

"You said you'd leave it on!" sobbed Anna-Magdalena, accusingly.

Mum squeezed her tight. "I'm really sorry. Sometimes *mums* need to be more careful too. We'll pray for that tomorrow night."

Anna-Magdalena wrapped her arms tightly round her mum, wanting to keep her sitting on the bed. Mum kissed her forehead and said, "When you feel frightened, don't forget that God loves you. He's looking after you at night, as well as in the day."

Anna-Magdalena nodded but now her eyelids felt very heavy. She lay back in her bed and was soon fast asleep.

Early the next evening Anna-Magdalena was playing ball with Patch, her tortoiseshell kitten. She had an orange patch on her head which was how she had got her name. Mum had just gone into the kitchen to cook the tea.

Suddenly all the lights went out!

Gerald, Anna-Magdalena's stepdad, was upstairs, putting Luke to bed. He shouted, "It must be a power cut!"

Anna-Magdalena's room was totally dark once more. She blew upon her fringe in a worried way. Her voice quavered as she called out to Gerald, "Wh-where are you?"

"I'm here on the landing, walking towards you. Follow my voice," he replied.

It wasn't nearly so bad with a voice to walk towards. Feeling her way around the bed and the door frame, Anna-Magdalena met Gerald on the landing. He took her hand.

"What's a power cut?" she asked. She felt perfectly safe now.

Gerald explained, "It means there's no electricity. Something goes wrong at the power station where they make the electricity and the lights go out and all electrical machines like cookers and fridges stop running."

They felt their way down the stairs and to the front door. They looked out. The whole street was black. No street lights, no lights at any of the windows.

"What we need are some candles," said Gerald. "Pauline, where are the candles?"

he called out into the darkness to Anna-Magdalena's mum.

"Aren't they by the fuse-box in the cellar?" she shouted from the kitchen. No, they weren't there.

"How about the sideboard?" she suggested next.

Gerald and Anna-Magdalena felt through the drawers. No, they weren't there.

Suddenly, it was as if a light went on in Anna-Magdalena's head. *She* remembered where the candles were.

"I know!" she exclaimed. In her excitement she forgot her fear of the dark. She left the safety of Gerald's side and felt her way round the sofa. Then she bumped into the table.

"Ouch!" she muttered. Anna-Magdalena felt round the table and into the hall downstairs. She opened the hall corner cupboard. There, on the bottom shelf, her fingers discovered a big box of candles.

"I've got the candles!" cried Anna-Magdalena. Back from the hall she came, carrying the box and feeling her way. She bumped into the table again and mumbled "Ouch," even though this time it didn't hurt. Patting with her free hand round the sofa, she got back to Gerald.

"I saw the candles before," explained Anna-Magdalena. "Patch chased her ball into the cupboard. The door was open."

"Well done!" said Gerald, scooping her up and giving her a big hug.

"That was brave of you," said Mum, who'd come in from the kitchen. She kissed Anna-Magdalena.

Mum lit a candle and the first thing she saw was Anna-Magdalena's big, pleased grin.

After that, Gerald and Mum lit lots of candles and stood them in holders all round the sitting-room. It looked lovely, all glowing and friendly. Gerald lit the coal fire and soon the fireplace was full of friendly flames.

"We've got light. We'll soon have more heat," said Gerald with satisfaction. "Now, what about our tea?"

"I'm hungry," Anna-Magdalena said.

Suddenly she felt very hungry indeed.

Mum said, "The cooker's electric, so that's useless. But I'll see what I can find." She took two candles with her into the kitchen. In a little while, she returned carrying a tray. On it were uncooked sausages, slices of bread, margarine, ketchup, tomatoes, crisps, jam, apples, chocolate biscuits and apple juice.

Gerald found a pocket torch and went out of the kitchen door. In a moment he was back with two green sticks he'd cut from the shrub outside. Using a penknife, he whittled a pointy end to each stick and handed one to Anna-Magdalena.

He showed her how to thread a sausage on to her stick. "Now hold it over the fire," he said.

Mum toasted bread on a toasting fork while Gerald and Anna-Magdalena did the sausages.

"Done yet?" Anna-Magdalena asked, inspecting her blackening sausage.

"Probably not," said Gerald. "Don't hold it so near the flames. Give the inside of the sausage time to cook too."

59

By the time Gerald declared the sausages finished, Anna-Magdalena felt cooked herself, sitting there in front of the warm fire.

They ate sausages in toast with drippy ketchup, and then had tomatoes and crisps. The sausages tasted slightly burnt, but Anna-Magdalena was so hungry she didn't care. After that they drank juice and munched toast and jam, apples and chocolate biscuits. It was a really lovely picnic.

Anna-Magdalena glanced round the softly lit room. She thought it had never looked so nice. It was really cosy to have her mum and Gerald sitting on cushions beside her on the floor by the fire. "Can we have tea like this tomorrow night?" she asked.

They laughed and promised that they would do it again the very next time there was a power cut.

"I hope the lights go out soon," said Anna-Magdalena. She thought for a moment. "'Cept in my room," she added.

Next day they went to the shops. Anna-Magdalena chose a wonderful new night lamp. It was a china teddybear in a pink china nightie and nightcap. The teddy was open at the back and held a little bulb. The light shone through holes round the neckline and hem of the teddy's nightie. Mum put it on a high shelf in the bedroom for safety.

Anna-Magdalena thought it was the best lamp she'd ever seen. And Bear promised not to be jealous of the new teddy.

The Leaning Silver Birch

JAMES RIORDAN

There once lived a man who was poor but as sharp as a bone needle. And in the same village lived a rich man who thought himself smarter than the night is black.

The rich man was walking along one time when he spotted his neighbour in the distance leaning against a tree.

Coming up to him, he said: "I have heard you possess the tongue of a magpie and the brain of a fox. But you cannot outwit me!"

"I could do so for sure," replied the

other. "But not right now, I've left my box of tricks at home."

The rich man gave a mocking laugh.

"Then run home and fetch it. I'll wait for you . . ."

"I would gladly do so," replied the other. "But you see, if I move away from this leaning silver birch, it will fall over."

The rich man grinned.

"Enough of your excuses! Just go and get your box of tricks. I'll hold up the tree till you get back."

And off went the quick-witted one, smiling to himself.

In the meantime the boaster waited and waited, holding up the tree. It was only when the villagers gathered to laugh at him that he realized he had been tricked. And never again did he boast about his quick wit.

Making Pancakes When My Mother was Out

PADDY KINSALE

It was all her own fault really; she said she wasn't going to make any pancakes this year because she hadn't got time. So when Sally and Bill came round I said it was all right for them, *they* could have pancakes for *their* tea but we couldn't have any for ours, Ruthie and me. Sally said, "Let's make 'em for her. I know how to do it."

"Yeah," said Bill. "Save her the trouble. I know how to make pancakes as well. You get some baking flour and mix it up with a

64

lot of eggs and sugar. I've seen my mum do it hundreds of times."

"I thought you had to have lard in it." I said.

"No," said Bill, "that's when you're making roly-polys – I think."

"Bet you don't know at all," I said.

"Stop it, Ruthie," I said, because she was trying to make a pancake of her own out of a piece of horrible old bread she had got hold of out of the waste bin. She always goes scrabbling about in our waste bin when your back is turned. She's only two so I suppose she doesn't know any better. Trouble is, she eats it if you don't watch her. Anyway, I thought it would be a good idea to make some pancakes for when mum came home. It would save her the trouble. So I agreed.

We got out a big dish and I climbed on a stool and reached the flour down from the cupboard, knocking the sugar over as I did it. That was the first accident. You know what sugar's like – it seems to get all over the place – in the bread and butter, all over the floor, and some of it was on

Ruthie's head. She didn't mind. She was licking it up as it trickled down her face.

We put some flour in the dish and scraped the sugar into it off the table. There were a few bread crumbs as well but we didn't think it would matter very much because, as Bill said, bread was made from flour anyway. Then Sally broke some eggs into it and dropped one on the floor. I was just going for the floor-cloth to get it up when Ruthie went and stood in it.

"Naughty girl!" I said, and she started to cry and backed away, bumping into Bill who was just taking the top off a bottle of milk so that it jerked his hand and the milk went everywhere, most of it all over my back, because I was kneeling down trying to get the egg up.

"I've got half an eggshell in this," Sally said. "I can't get it out." She was trying to fish it out with a pencil, and the more she fished the further it got stuck in the goo.

"Oh, leave it," Bill said. "We can pull it out when the things are cooking in the frying-pan."

66

So Sally started to stir it up but it didn't look right at all.

"It's the milk that needs putting in it," Bill said and poured this pint of milk as Sally had just let go of the pencil, so that she had to stick her hand in it to get the pencil out.

"Ugh!" she said. "Horrible and sticky!" waving her hand about in the air and milk and blobs of egg and stuff were flying about. Bill started laughing and leaned back – right on the two eggs that were left on the table.

"Ughowgh!" he said when he saw yellow sticky egg all over his sleeve. "Ughowgh," said Ruthie, imitating him and watching the egg drip off the table into her hand.

"Come out, you lot," I said. "Mum'll go mad." I managed to wipe most of the egg with a tea towel which I hid behind the sink. Sally had found a spoon at last and was stirring up the sickly looking mixture. We all peered at it with wrinkled noses.

"Think it'll be all right," I said.

"Looks a bit scrobbly," Bill said. It was

all sort of sloppy with big gobbets of eggy flour floating about in it.

"Funny," Sally said. "Doesn't look like that when my mom does it. Perhaps we should put some salt in it."

So I got this plastic salt container which has a little cap at the top to stop the salt from rushing out all at once, but there must have been something the matter with it because as I tipped it up the top came off and about half a pound of salt wooshed into the mixture. The plastic cap just sank like a stone in a pond. We all looked at it.

"Won't taste very nice now, will it?" said Bill.

"Well, put some sugar in it so the salt won't be noticed," Sally said. Bill then emptied the rest of the sugar into the mixture and Sally went on stirring. We forgot all about the cap. "I think it's ready now," Sally said. We got the frying-pan on the stove and turned up the heat. Then Sally poured in some of the stuff and flattened the lumps down a bit, but instead of just cooking it started to let out squeaks and a terrible smoke, and within seconds the kitchen was so full you could hardly see anything. I was trying to open the window and accidentally knocked the handle of the frying-pan so that it pitched out the evil-looking mess of a pancake onto the floor. Some of it went on Bill's shoe and some stuck to the stove and began to go black and send out more smoke. We were so busy trying to get it up, opening the door, turning off the stove and waving the smoke out with newspapers and the lid of the bread bin, that nobody noticed that Ruthie had got the basin in the corner and was slopping out what was left of the mixture in great handfuls into *my* wellingtons.

That was when mum came in. I try to forget what happened after that, but a big black gloom came down on the scene. We all decided later that cooking wasn't really in our line.

The Pearl Tree

IRA SAXENA

Once upon a time, there lived a poor priest, Shivam, in the kingdom of Chandrasen. Shivam performed religious ceremonies on the occasion of the birth of a child, a marriage or a death in a family. He took whatever people offered and never asked for more. His earnings were just enough for an ordinary living. He led a simple life, ate plain food and slept on a mat of dried palm leaves.

Shivam was happy, but his wife, Manjari, was very dissatisfied. She wanted nice clothes to wear, a wooden bed, an ornamental swing to relax upon and plenty of rice to give in charity. By feeding the hungry, she believed, they would become lucky and prosperous.

Every day she coaxed her husband, "Why don't you go to King Chandrasen. Everyone says he is kind-hearted and charitable. He never refuses anything to priests. Ask him for a barrel of rice and a pouch of gold coins. Then we will never need anything else, we will live comfortably."

And every day Shivam would give the same answer, "Why should I go there, when there is no occasion for my services, I won't accept charity. There's enough for both of us, so be content."

But, his arguments did not convince Manjari. She wanted the barrel of rice for charity and gold to buy the things she wanted.

One day, the King's drummers came to the town and read out the King's message: "The land has given a large crop, the forests are lush and green and the cows give plenty of milk in our kingdom. There is prosperity everywhere. To celebrate, the

71

King has invited all the priests to the palace."

When Manjari heard this she thought her prayers had been answered. She forced her husband to go to the King's palace. Shivam agreed because the King had sent the invitation.

At the palace, Shivam sat with the other priests of the kingdom. In his flowing brocade robes King Chandrasen came and distributed silk shawls, rice and gold coins to everyone. When he came to Shivam and offered the gifts, Shivam joined his palms and thanked him politely:

"O gracious King, thank you, but I cannot take anything because I have not performed any ritual or chanted prayers for you. That is my job and until I have worked I can't accept anything, either grain or gold."

King Chandrasen was very pleased to hear such noble words. He wanted to shower the simple man with gifts. At the same time, respecting Shivam's principles, the King requested, "Please, sing a prayer for my welfare!"

Shivam did as he was told. After the prayer, King Chandrasen offered the gifts to him, but Shivam shook his head.

"Thank you, O gracious King. This is too much for what I have done. Just give me four paise, that's all I can accept."

King Chandrasen was very impressed. he joined his palms, bowed before Shivam and offered four paise.

Again Shivam declined and said, "O King, I want four paise out of your earnings. This money has come from your treasury which contains the wealth collected by taxes. It is actually the toil of your people, not your own hard-earned money."

The King was dumbfounded. It was true, not a single penny in his treasury came from his labour. But he was not disheartened. He joined his palms again and requested, "Give me two days and I will give you four paise of my labour."

"Certainly, I will return in two days time," said Shivam and took his leave.

At home, Manjari was waiting impatiently to grab all the riches from her husband.

When she saw him enter empty-handed, she was furious. Only when Shivam told her that he would be going to the palace again did she settle down.

Meanwhile, at the palace, King Chandrasen was lost deep in thought. He did not know how to earn the four paise. The more he thought, the more he realized that he could not do anything at all. Even his own work was done by his servants. However, having resolved to earn the money, King Chandrasen disguised himself as a poor man and left the palace in search of work.

King Chandrasen could not find any work in the town. He could not stitch shoes, wash clothes, sand the wood or even pull a cart steadily. Wherever he went he was refused work, but he did not give up. At last, he saw a wealthy merchant waiting for his servant.

"Can I do some work for you, Sire?" asked King Chandrasen.

The merchant looked at his tattered clothes and took pity on him. "Go on," he

74

said and, pointing towards the earthen pitcher, ordered, "take the pitcher, fetch water from the well and fill the tub."

King Chandrasen was very pleased. Quickly, he went to the well and started pulling up the water. It was hard work. When he set off with the full, heavy pitcher, it was still harder. After every couple of steps he would falter and almost fall. Slowly and with great difficulty King Chandrasen carried four pitchers of water to the tub. He was very tired and sweaty. As he carried the fifth pitcher, he couldn't remain steady and he dropped the pitcher. The pitcher broke into bits and the water spilled everywhere.

Disgusted, the merchant shouted, "Goodness me, what a good-for-nothing fellow! You can't even fetch water properly," and looking fed up he said, "Here, take it, one paisa for each pitcher of water you brought, now get lost."

Quietly King Chandrasen took the four paise and wiped the sweat from his brow. "Whew!" he panted. "It is indeed tough to earn money," he said to himself.

The next day he offered the four paise to Shivam. "This is the gift of my hard work, now you can't refuse it." Shivam took it happily and left.

At home, Manjari was eagerly waiting for her husband, dreaming of rich silks, sacks of rice and glittering gold which he would bring with him. When Shivam gave her the four paise, she went into a rage and shouted at him, "Everyone got silks and gold and the King gave you only four paise. What have I done to deserve this?" She wept and asked, "Couldn't you have asked for more?"

"That's all I wanted. These are the most precious four paise," Shivam explained mildly. But Manjari was furious. Angrily, she threw the four paise in the garden.

After some time four plants sprang in their garden. As time went by, the plants turned into beautiful trees that bore bunches of golden pearls. Loads and loads of pearls grew every day and scattered in the courtyard. Each pearl shone like golden rays of the sun, the glitter was heavenly. Never had anyone seen such pearls.

Manjari did not throw them away. Every morning she swept them into the shed. Gradually the small heap grew into a mountain of glowing pearls.

One day the vegetable woman's little daughter saw them and asked, "Will you give me some for my necklace?"

Manjari picked a handful and gave it to her, but her mother refused. "I can't take it for free. Let me give you some vegetables in payment for the pearls."

Manjari was delighted to find some use for the pearls from the trees. From then onwards, every day she purchased vegetables in exchange for the pearls. In the same way she purchased other things she needed. Very soon, she bought a wooden bed, an ornamental swing, lots of new clothes for herself and her husband and plenty of rice to give in charity. Manjari became very happy.

One day, Princess Ratna was travelling through the town. As she looked out of her carriage, she was enchanted by the glitter of the golden pearls that the women in town were wearing. She had never seen such beautiful pearls. The princess yearned for them, and she returned to the palace looking sad.

When King Chandrasen asked what the reason for her sadness was, she said, "All I want is a garland of golden pearls, like the ones I've seen." The King smiled at the princess fondly and ordered his soldiers to find out about the pearls.

When the soldiers returned with a pearl, even King Chandrasen was bewitched by its glow. And when they told him that the pearls grew on trees, the King could not believe it.

"Incredible!" he said and announced, "Prepare the carriage, I will go and see the pearl tree for myself."

In a short while, King Chandrasen and Princess Ratna were at the doorstep of Shivam's simple cottage. Both Shivam and Manjari were delighted to be able to welcome them.

The King and Princess entered and gazed at the four trees and the mountain of glowing pearls in the shed; they were absolutely wonderstruck. "Tell me your price, I wish to buy all the pearls for my daughter," the King addressed Shivam and Manjari.

"These trees belong to you, O King. How can we give you a price?" both replied humbly.

"I don't understand," King Chandrasen looked confused.

"Do you remember when you worked hard to earn four paise in order to give them to me?" Shivam asked. Manjari explained further, "I threw those four paise in anger, right where the trees stand. Little did I know that those four paise would bear such wonderful fruit. They have given us everything we have ever wanted."

"These pearls are the sweat of your brow, O worthy King," concluded Shivam.

But the King found it hard to believe. He told his soldiers to dig to the roots of the trees. They started digging and found that the tree was cropping out of a paisa coin. King Chandrasen recognized it.

Bewildered, he thought aloud, "Just one hour of labour creates such beautiful results," and he said to the Princess, "Go on, dear, take all you need for your garland. It is, indeed, my real gift to you."

"Yes, Father, the best gift a king could give to his daughter," said Princess Ratna lovingly and started collecting the glowing pearls in her basket.

Careless Conrad

M. JOYCE DAVIES

Conrad Cluckerty was a young chicken. He was in most ways quite a good little chicken – except that he was always losing things. He lost his shoes, and his cap, and his hankies, and his school books and pencils, and sometimes even his pocket money. And then of course, he had to stop and look for the things he had lost. He had to search in cupboards and drawers, under all the furniture, and in all his pockets, and that usually took ages and ages – so he was nearly always late and hurrying to try to catch up with the time he had lost searching for things.

"Always behind, like the cow's tail!" his Mother said.

One day Conrad was late for tea, as he very often was.

"What makes you so late today, Conrad?" asked his Mother.

"I lost my cap," answered Conrad, "and I had to stop and look for it."

"Oh Conrad, Conrad," sighed his Mother, "what a careless chicken you are. Why can't you learn to be more careful? It's a good job your head doesn't take off, or you'd probably lose that, too."

"Yes, Mother," said Conrad meekly, while his little sister giggled at the thought of Conrad searching for his own head.

"Now be quick and finish your tea," said Mrs Cluckerty. "I want you to run an errand for me."

"Yes, Mother," said Conrad again. Then he found he had lost his teaspoon, and he had to get down and look under the table for it.

"I want you to go and post this letter

for me," said Mrs Cluckerty, when Conrad had finished his tea, "and I want it most particularly to catch the last post this evening. I've only just remembered that it is your Great Uncle Crowster's birthday tomorrow, and if he doesn't get this letter in the morning he'll think we have forgotten him. So just you run along with it to the post office, Conrad. Here's the money for you to buy a stamp – and don't lose it! Wait a minute, wait a minute!" she called, as Conrad seized the money and was dashing off. "You haven't got the letter yet, you silly chicken. There now," she continued, as she handed him the letter, "there's no need to go tearing off like a mad thing. There's plenty of time to get there and back twice over before the post goes out. Just you go steadily and do try not to lose anything."

Conrad took the letter carefully in one hand and held the money in the other. "If I keep tight hold of them like this I can't lose them!" he thought. He hadn't gone very far when he saw Flossie Flatfoot, his duckling friend, a little way away. Flossie waved to him.

"Hi, Conrad!" she called. "Where are you off to in such a hurry?"

"I've got to catch the post!" shouted Conrad.

"Well, you don't need to be in such a tearing hurry about it," answered Flossie. "See, I've got some pop-corn here – have some!" and she ran towards him, holding up a big bag of luscious pop-corn.

"Oo!" breathed Conrad. "Oo, Flossie, I do love pop-corn!"

"So do I," agreed Flossie; "let's sit down and eat some."

"I mustn't stay more than three minutes, then," said Conrad hesitating.

"We can eat a lot of pop-corn in three minutes," laughed Flossie.

They both sat down on the broad stretch of grass by the side of the road, and Flossie held the bag out for Conrad to help himself. Then Conrad found he was in a difficulty. He had the letter in one hand and the money for the stamp in the other, that meant he had not got a hand to spare to take any pop-corn.

"I've got to be specially careful not to

lose these," he said, holding up the letter and the money to show Flossie.

"Couldn't you just put the letter down a minute, and put the money in your pocket while we eat the pop-corn," she suggested.

So Conrad did as she said, and he *did* enjoy that pop-corn.

"Well now I must be getting on," he said, after ten minutes or so.

"All right," answered Flossie, "I'll go along with you." So they both jumped up and set off for the post office. Conrad started off at a run, but Flossie had no intention of going with him at that pace. "There's not all that tremendous hurry, Conrad," she protested, "It's only quite a little way to the post office from here."

"Yes, I know," admitted Conrad, slowing down his pace to match Flossie's, "but I'm so afraid I may forget where it is I have to go."

"I'll remind you, don't you worry," she promised him.

At the post office door Conrad said good-bye to Flossie and hurried in to buy his stamp. Then he realized to his dismay that he was no longer holding the money in his hand – but he suddenly remembered that he had slipped it into his pocket while he ate the pop-corn.

Feeling much relieved he felt in his coat pocket. He felt in one pocket – then in another – and another – then in his trousers pockets, but it was no good – the money wasn't there – he must have LOST it! He felt carefully once more, in case there were any pockets he had forgotten, but there were not any. He racked his brains to try to remember which pocket he had put the money in, but it was no good – he just hadn't any idea.

"Oh dear, oh dear!" sighed Conrad, "whatever shall I do?"

He started to turn all the things out of his pockets – no money. He turned all his pockets inside out – still no money. He took off his jacket and turned it upside down and shook it – that wasn't any good either; he was just putting it on again sadly, when he heard something chinking in the front corner between the lining and the jacket. Feverishly he felt to see what it was – it was the money for the stamp. There must have been a hole in the lining of his pocket, and the coins had fallen through.

With a little trouble he managed to get the money back again through the hole in the pocket; then, overjoyed that he hadn't lost anything *this* time, he bought the stamp.

But his joy was short-lived. To be sure he had the stamp all right, but where was the letter to stick it on to? It wasn't any use searching through his pockets again, he'd done that already, and he knew there wasn't any letter there. Then he remembered! He had put the letter down on the grass while he sat eating pop-corn with Flossie; he must have forgotten to pick it up again!

Off he ran, as fast as he could go, back to the place where they had been sitting. Anxiously he searched about, for a time with no success, then at last he spied something white in the long grass near the hedge. He pounced on it, and there – oh rapture – was the letter! It looked, perhaps, just a trifle grubby, but it was quite safe. Now he had only to stick the stamp on, and then run back with it to the post.

But where was the stamp? Whatever had he done with it? He racked his brains to remember when he saw it last. He remembered buying it – and then putting the things back in his pockets – and then looking for the letter – and then – why, of course, his pockets! It must be in one of his pockets; he must search again.

By this time he was getting cautious, he was a bit tired of searching for things, so he placed the letter carefully on the ground and put his foot on it before he started to examine his pockets.

"I can't lose it if I keep standing on it," he thought, as he started to turn out the contents of his pockets. He turned out two marbles, an empty matchbox, a rather grubby hankie, three acorns, a red button, various odds and ends of string, and a sticky paper bag that once seemed to have held some sweets – but no stamp. Conrad placed all the things on the ground in front of him and examined them carefully, one by one. He was going through them for the third time, and had just decided that the paper bag was too crumpled to be worth keeping, when something hidden in one of its creases caught his eye. Hurrah! The stamp at last!

Conrad separated the stamp from the sticky folds of the bag with great care, and fixed it firmly on the corner of the letter. He heaved a sigh; that was all right. Just let him put the things back in his pockets, then run with the letter to the post, and there would be no more worry.

But alas! This time Conrad had forgotten to put his foot on the letter when he placed it on the ground, in order to put the things back into his pockets. As he was stuffing the last piece of string into his trousers pocket a sudden gust of wind sprang up, and – swish – away sailed the letter, stamp and all, over a nearby hedge.

Poor Conrad! He searched frantically for a hole in the hedge, and when at last he found one big enough to scramble through, the letter was whirling merrily about over the far side of the field.

"Come back! Come back!" he panted as he dashed across the field. It seemed almost as if the letter heard him, for it fluttered down, and lay for a moment on the grass; then, just as Conrad rushed up and reached out to pick it off the ground – *whoo* – another gust of wind lifted it, and away it soared into the next field.

Up hill and down dale the wind carried that letter, always just ahead of poor Conrad as he panted on and on, not looking where he was going, but thinking only of one thing – *he must not lose that letter!*

At length, when it seemed to him that he must have run miles and miles, and he felt he could go no farther, the playful breeze dropped as suddenly as it had sprung up, the letter floated gently to the ground and Conrad flung himself on top of it, out of breath and exhausted.

For some minutes he lay still, wondering if he would ever get his breath back again. Then he remembered that he still had to *post* the letter.

"Well," he thought, as he sat up, grasping the letter in both hands. "Well, I certainly haven't lost anything, but I've got a long way to go to get back to the post, so I s'pose I'd better get going."

He scrambled to his feet and looked around for the way home. But he had followed the letter farther than he realized, and he found himself in a lonely, deserted bit of country, where he had never been before.

He was on a wild open common, with nothing except a few scrubby bushes, and odd patches of bracken to be seen in any direction. "I wish I could see someone about, so that I could ask the way," thought Conrad, as he looked around him, this way and then that way, but there was no sign of anyone, or even a house anywhere so far as it was possible for him to see. He even tried looking up at the sky – but that wasn't any good either – there wasn't so much as a bird to be seen. "I wonder which will be the quickest way home," he mused, with a worried look, "perhaps if I walk on a bit I shall come to some place I know, and then I shall be all right. But which way shall I walk – I-I don't know!" Conrad turned slowly round peering in every direction in turn, but nowhere could he see one single sign of anything he remembered having seen before. Still, he simply must go in *some* direction, and that as quickly as possible. "I think I came this way," he said to himself firmly, as he set off. Then, after a few yards, he halted. "Or was it that way?" he wondered doubtfully. He tried to recognize some landmark he might have passed as he chased after the letter, but in whatever direction he turned the place looked much the same, just open meadow-land without any distinguishing feature anywhere in sight.

"Oh dear," he thought sadly, "I believe I have lost something after all; I'm afraid I've lost my way!"

He turned himself round, looking anxiously for some tree or bush which might guide him back the way he had come. But he could see nothing to help him.

"It's no use standing here," he decided at last. "I shall never catch the post that way. It must be getting very late; I'll just go straight ahead until I come to something I can recognize."

So off he marched, looking all about him as he went, but still he couldn't see any familiar landmark; he didn't even know if he was going in the right direction. Suddenly an awful idea came to him.

"I've not only lost my way," he thought in dismay, "I've lost MYSELF!"

This was truly a dismal thought, for with all the things he kept on losing, he had never ever lost himself before, and he couldn't, for the life of him, think how he ought to set about finding himself. He was puzzling what to do about it when a shadow fell across his path. He looked up and saw to his horror, the grinning face and shining white teeth of Mr FOX. For a moment Conrad's heart stood still with fear, then he turned and fled.

He had run fast before, but he ran even faster now, as he heard Mr Fox padding after him and heard his horrid low chuckle. Conrad knew quite well he couldn't keep that pace up for long; Mr Fox was gaining on him he could tell, and he looked desperately round for a hiding-place.

There was an old hollow tree-trunk lying on the ground close by. Panting and trembling, Conrad rushed at it and wriggled his way inside – it was too small for Mr Fox to follow.

As Conrad began to recover his breath, he also began to wonder what to do next. He was inside the tree-trunk, safe for the moment, but how was he going to get out? Mr Fox was just outside licking his lips and Conrad had often heard his Mother tell how partial Mr Fox was to a nice tender young chicken for supper. And with Mr Fox outside how was he to post the letter, which he still held clutched tightly in his hand. And even if Mr Fox wasn't there he didn't know the way home to the post. Conrad felt that now indeed everything was lost.

Then suddenly he cocked his head on one side and listened. Was it? Yes, it was! Faint at first, but coming nearer, he heard the sound of barking. It was the most welcome sound he had ever heard, *and* it was a bark that he knew well. It belonged to no less a person than Shippy, the farmyard dog, a great friend of all Conrad's family.

"Shippy!" shouted Conrad with all the strength of his lungs. "Save me! It's me, Conrad! Oh! save me, Shippy, save me!"

The entrance to his tree-trunk seemed to grow lighter, and Conrad saw to his joy, that Mr Fox was no longer waiting for him outside. Mr Fox was galloping away as fast as he could go. Shippy was no friend of *his*.

Conrad crept out of the hollow trunk with a squeak of delight as Shippy bounded up.

"Oh Shippy," he gasped. "Oh Shippy dear, it is good to see you!"

"Conrad!" wuffed Shippy in surprise: "What are you doing here?"

Conrad told Shippy the whole story; how he had lost first the money, then the letter, and the stamp, and then the letter again. How he had chased after the letter for what seemed like miles, and miles, and how terribly frightened he had been when he saw Mr Fox, and found that he had lost

95

himself, and how very, very, very glad he was to see dear old Shippy, and he finished up, "and, oh Shippy, I haven't posted Mother's letter yet; have I lost the last post, do you think?"

"I don't know," answered Shippy, "It may not have gone out yet – there may be just time to catch it. If you jump up on my back I'll do my best."

Conrad jumped on to Shippy's back and held on tight as the old sheepdog bounded away. They went so fast that it made Conrad feel giddy; he felt sure he had never travelled so fast in his life before. He shut his eyes, clutched his letter tightly to him, and clung on to Shippy's collar.

"Nearly there now!" barked Shippy at last. Conrad opened his eyes and found himself in the old familiar market-place, with the post office over in the farthest corner. And there was the postman just clearing the postbox for the last collection.

Shippy barked and Conrad chirped as loud as ever they could. The postman looked up and saw them just as he was closing his bag; he noticed the letter in

Conrad's hand and opened his bag again for it to be dropped in.

Shippy bounded up to the postman, and stood with his tongue hanging out, panting, while Conrad leaned from his back and with a sigh of relief, dropped his precious letter among all the other letters in the post-bag. "Running it a bit fine, aren't you, my lad?" asked the postman as he closed the bag and slung it over his shoulder. "You very nearly lost the last post *that* time!"

"I didn't quite lose it though," said Conrad, as he patted Shippy's head, "but I should have done if it hadn't been for good old Shippy."

How happy Conrad felt as they turned towards home. He still rode on Shippy's back, but they went at a more sedate pace now.

"Why, Conrad," exclaimed his Mother, as they arrived at the Cluckertys' house, "I was beginning to think you'd got lost."

"So I did, Mother," squeaked Conrad, "but Shippy found me again, and I haven't lost *anything* this time!"

He told his Mother all about his adventures, how he had so nearly lost so many things, and had managed to find them again, "and in the end I didn't even lose the post!" he finished triumphantly.

"Well, it certainly seems to have been your lucky day," said his Mother, "but you *must* try to be more careful. You won't always be so lucky, you know, and you won't always have Shippy come to rescue you."

"No, Mother, I know," answered Conrad. "I *will* try to be careful in future." And to prove his words, he managed to save up two whole weeks' pocket money without losing it, and he bought a lovely bone as a present for Shippy.

How Trouble Made the Monkey Eat Pepper

GRACE HALLWORTH

An old woman used to buy molasses from a nearby village. One day as she was returning home she tripped over the roots of a tree and her calabash fell and broke, spilling the molasses she had just bought.

When the old woman saw her molasses running on the ground and going to waste she began to cry:

*"Lordie, Lordie, look at mi trouble, oui
Lordie, Lordie, how trouble overtake me!"*

She scooped up as much of the molasses

as she could with a bit of broken calabash and continued on her way. As soon as she had gone, Monkey climbed down from the tree where he had seen and heard all that had happened.

He sniffed the treacly, sweet syrup on the ground and in no time he had licked it all up.

"Yum, yum!" he said, smacking his lips, "if this is trouble then I'll have double." And off he ran to the village shop to buy some trouble.

Now when Monkey entered the shop and asked for double trouble, the shopkeeper could make neither head nor tail of it. So Monkey explained what had happened to the old woman. Then the shopkeeper saw his chance of getting even with Monkey, who had pelted him with coconuts the last time he had taken a short cut through the forest.

He went to the back of the shop, seized two bulldogs sleeping there and put them into a sack which he tied securely. Then he returned to the shop and handed the sack to Monkey.

"There's enough trouble in here to keep you busy for quite a while," said the shopkeeper.

Without so much as an "If you please," or a "Thank you," Monkey threw the money down on the counter, grabbed the sack and rushed off. He ran deep, deep into the forest until he came to a quiet shady patch under a gru-gru palm where he sat down and made ready to·enjoy trouble. No sooner had he opened the sack than the two bulldogs jumped out and rushed to attack him. Monkey barely had time to leap to a branch of the gru-gru palm, and there he crouched, not daring to move, the hot sun burning into his skin and the thorns digging into his paws and the bulldogs baying and barking at the foot of the tree.

Thus it was that the shopkeeper found Monkey late, late that evening when he went to look for his dogs.

*"Ah Monkey! What trouble is this I see.
Double trouble wait under this tree!"*

said the shopkeeper.

Poor Monkey was so faint and weak he could hardly speak. Growing quite near was a pepper tree laden with red-hot peppers. He had eaten nothing all day and peppers, even red-hot peppers, were better than nothing. Monkey reached out and devoured pepper after pepper until there wasn't a pepper left on the tree.

Tears ran down his face and as the pepper burned his tongue, his mouth and his stomach, Monkey gasped:

"I have had my fill of trouble,
Hungry and thirsty I'm seeing double."

"Then," said the shopkeeper, "take my advice, Monkey, and never trouble trouble unless trouble trouble you."

The Tortoises' Picnic

KATHERINE BRIGGS

There were once three tortoises – a father, a mother and a baby. And one fine spring day they decided that they would like to go for a picnic. They picked the place they would go to, a nice wood at some distance off, and they began to get their stuff together. They got tins of salmon and tins of tongue, and sandwiches, and orange squash, and everything they could think of. In about three months they were ready, and they set out, carrying their baskets.

They walked and walked and walked, and time went on, and after about eighteen months they sat down and had a rest. But they knew just where they wanted to go and they were about half way to it, so they set out again. And in three years they reached the picnic place. They unpacked their baskets and spread out the cloth, and arranged the food on it and it looked lovely.

Then Mother Tortoise began to look into the picnic baskets. She turned them all upside down, and shook them, but they were all empty, and at last she said, "We've forgotten the tin-opener!" They looked at each other, and at last Father and Mother said, "Baby, you'll have to go back for it."

"What!" said the baby, "me! Go back all that long way!"

"Nothing for it," said Father Tortoise, "we can't start without a tin-opener. We'll wait for you."

"Well, do you swear, do you promise faithfully," said the baby, "that you won't touch a thing till I come back?"

"Yes, we promise faithfully," they said, and Baby plodded away, and after a while he was lost to sight among the bushes.

And Father and Mother waited. They waited and waited and waited, and a whole year went by, and they began to get rather hungry. But they'd promised, so they waited. And another year went by, and another, and they got really hungry.

"Don't you think we could have just one sandwich each?" said Mother Tortoise. "He'd never know the difference."

"No," said Father Tortoise, "we promised. We must wait till he comes back."

So they waited, and another year passed, and another, and they got ravenous.

"It's six years now," said Mother Tortoise. "He ought to be back by now."

"Yes, I suppose he ought," said Father Tortoise. "Let's just have one sandwich while we're waiting."

They picked up the sandwiches, but just as they were going to eat them, a little voice said, "Aha! I knew you'd cheat." And Baby Tortoise popped his head out of a bush. "It's a good thing I didn't start for that tin-opener," he said.

In the Beginning and Pandora's Box

GERALDINE McCAUGHREAN

At the very beginning, the gods ruled over an empty world. From their home on Mount Olympus, where they lived in halls of sunlight and cloud, they looked out over oceans and islands, woodland and hill. But nothing moved in the landscape because there were no animals or birds or people.

Zeus, king of the gods, gave Prometheus and his brother Epimetheus the task of making living creatures, and he sent them down to live on earth. Epimetheus made turtles and gave them shells; he made horses and gave them tails and manes. He made anteaters and gave them long noses and longer tongues; he made birds and gave them the gift of flight. But although Epimetheus was a wonderful craftsman, he was not nearly as clever as his brother. So Prometheus watched over his brother's work and, when all the animals and birds, insects and fishes were made, it was Prometheus who made the very last creature of all. He took soil and mixed it into mud, and out of that he moulded First Man.

"I'll make him just like us gods – two legs, two arms and upright – not crawling on all fours. All the other beasts spend their days looking at the ground, but Man will look at the stars!"

When he had finished, Prometheus was very proud of what he had made. But when it came to giving Man a gift, there was nothing left to give!

"Give him a tail," said Epimetheus. But all the tails had gone. "Give him a trunk," Epimetheus suggested. But the elephant already had that. "Give him fur," said Epimetheus, but all the fur had been used up.

Suddenly Prometheus exclaimed, "I know what to give him!" He climbed up to heaven – up as high as the fiery chariot of the sun. And from the rim of its bright wheel he stole one tiny sliver of fire. It was such a very small flame that he was able to hide it inside a stalk of grass and hurry back to the earth without any of the gods seeing what he was up to.

But the secret could not be kept for long. Next time Zeus looked down from Mount Olympus, he saw something glimmering red and yellow under a column of grey smoke.

"Prometheus, what have you done? You've given the secret of fire to those . . . those . . . mud-men! Bad enough that you make them look like gods, now you go sharing our belongings with them! So! You put your little mud-people before us, do you? I'll make you sorry you ever made them! I'll make you sorry you ever made yourself!"

And he tied Prometheus to a cliff and sent eagles to peck at him all day long. You or I would have died. But the gods can never die. Prometheus knew that the pain would never end, that the eagles would never stop and that his chains would never break. A terrible hopelessness tore at his heart and hurt him more than the eagles could ever do.

Zeus was just as angry with Man for *accepting* the gift of fire, but you would never have thought so. He was busy making him another wonderful present.

With the help of the other gods, he shaped First Woman. Venus gave her beauty, Mercury gave her a clever tongue, Apollo taught her how to play sweet music. Finally Zeus draped a veil over her lovely head and named her Pandora.

Then, with a grin on his face, he sent for Epimetheus (who was not quite clever enough to suspect a trick).

"Here's a bride for you, Epimetheus – a reward for all your hard work making the animals. And here's a wedding present for you both. But whatever you do, don't open it."

The wedding present was a wooden chest, bolted and padlocked and bound with bands of iron. When he reached his home at the foot of Mount Olympus, Epimetheus set the chest down in a dark corner, covered it with a blanket, and put it out of his mind. After all, with Pandora for a bride, what more could a man possibly want?

In those days the world was a wonderful place to live. No one was sad. Nobody ever grew old or ill. And Epimetheus married Pandora; she came to live in his house, and everything she wanted he gave her.

But sometimes, when she caught sight of the chest, Pandora would say, "What a strange wedding present. Why can't we open it?"

"Never mind why. Remember, you must never touch it," Epimetheus would reply sharply. "Not touch at all. Do you hear?"

"Of course I won't touch it. It's only an old chest. What do I want with an old chest? . . . What do you think is inside?"

"Never mind what's inside. Put it out of your mind."

And Pandora did try. She really did. But one day, when Epimetheus was out, she just could not forget about the chest and somehow she found herself standing right beside it.

"No!" she told herself. "I expect it's full of cloth – or dishes – or papers. Something dull." She bustled about the house. She tried to read. Then . . .

"*Let us out!*"

"Who said that?"

"Do let us out, Pandora!"

Pandora looked out of the window. But in her heart of hearts she knew that the voice was coming from the chest. She pulled back the blanket with finger and thumb. The voice was louder now: "Please, please *do* let us out, Pandora!"

"I can't. I mustn't." She crouched down beside the chest.

"Oh, but you *have* to. We *want* you to. We *need* you to, Pandora!"

"But I promised!" Her fingers stroked the latch.

"It's easy. The key's in the lock," said the little voice – a purring little voice.

It was. A big golden key.

"No. No, I mustn't," she told herself.

111

"But you do *want* to, Pandora. And why shouldn't you? It was your wedding present too, wasn't it? . . . Oh, all right, don't let us out. Just peep inside. What harm can that do?"

Pandora's heart beat faster.

Click. The key turned.

Clack. Clack. The latches were unlatched.

BANG!

The lid flew back and Pandora was knocked over by an icy wind full of grit. It filled the room with howling. It tore the curtains and stained them brown. And after the wind came slimy things, growling snarling things, claws and snouts, revolting things too nasty to look at, all slithering out of the chest.

"I'm Disease," said one.

"I'm Cruelty," said another.

"I'm Pain, and she's Old Age."

"I'm Disappointment and he's Hate."

"I'm Jealousy and that one there is War."

"AND I AM DEATH!" said the smallest purring voice.

The creatures leapt and scuttled and oozed out through the windows, and at once all the flowers shrivelled, and the fruit on the trees grew mouldy. The sky itself turned a filthy yellow, and the sound of crying filled the town.

Mustering all her strength, Pandora slammed down the lid of the chest. But there was one creature left inside.

"No, no, Pandora! If you shut me inside, that will be your worst mistake of all! Let me go!"

"Oh no! You don't fool me twice," sobbed Pandora.

"But I am Hope!" whispered the little voice faintly. "Without me the world won't be able to bear all the unhappiness you have turned loose!"

So Pandora lifted the lid, and a white flicker, small as a butterfly, flitted out and was blown this way and that by the howling winds. And as it fluttered through the open window, a watery sun came out and shone on the wilted garden.

Chained to his cliff, Prometheus could do nothing to help the little mud-people he had made. Though he writhed and strained, there was no breaking free. All around him he could hear the sound of crying. Now that the snarling creatures had been let loose, there would be no more easy days or peaceful nights for men and women! They would be unkind, afraid, greedy, unhappy. And one day they must all die and go to live as ghosts in the cold dark Underworld. The thought of it almost broke Prometheus's heart.

Then, out of the corner of his eye, he glimpsed a little white flicker of light and felt something, small as a butterfly, touch his bare breast. Hope came to rest over his heart.

He felt a sudden strength, a sort of courage. He was sure that his life was not over. "No matter how bad things are today, tomorrow may be better," he thought. "One day someone may come this way – take pity on me – break these chains and set me free. One day!"

The eagles pecked at the fluttering shred of light but were too slow to catch it in their beaks. Hope fluttered on its way,

blowing round the world like a single tiny
tongue of flame.

The Crooked Little Finger

PHILIPPA PEARCE

One morning Judy woke up with a funny feeling in her little finger. It didn't exactly hurt; but it was beginning to ache and it was beginning to itch. It felt wrong. She held it straight out, and it still felt wrong. She curved it in on itself, with all the other fingers, and it still felt wrong.

In the end, she got dressed and went down to breakfast, holding that little finger straight up in the air, quite separately.

She sat down to breakfast, and said to her mother and her father and to her big brother, David, and her young sister, Daisy: "My little finger's gone wrong."

David asked: "What have you done to it?"

"Nothing," said Judy. "I just woke up this morning and it somehow felt wrong."

Her mother said: "I expect you'll wake up tomorrow morning and it'll somehow feel right."

"What about today though?" asked Judy; but her mother wasn't listening any more.

Her father said: "You haven't broken a bone in your little finger, have you, Judy? Can you bend it? Can you crook it – like this – as though you were beckoning with it?"

"Yes," said Judy; and then: "Ooooow!"

"Did it hurt, then?" said her mother, suddenly listening again, and anxious.

"No," said Judy. "It didn't hurt at all when I crooked it. But it felt *very* funny. It felt wrong. I didn't like it."

David said: "I'm tired of Judy's little finger," and their mother said: "Forget your little finger, Judy, and get on with your breakfast."

So Judy stopped talking about her little finger, but she couldn't forget it. It felt so odd. She tried crooking it again, and discovered that it wanted to crook itself. That was what it had been aching to do and itching to do.

She crooked it while she poured milk on her cereal and then waited for David to finish with the sugar.

Suddenly –

"Hey!" David cried angrily. "Don't *do* that, Judy!"

"What is it now?" exclaimed their mother, startled.

"She snatched the sugar from under my nose, just when I was helping myself." He was still holding the sugar spoon up in the air.

"I didn't!" said Judy.

"You did!" said David. "How else did the sugar get from me to you like that?"

"I crooked my little finger at it," said Judy.

David said: "What rubbish!" and their mother said: "Pass the sugar back to David at once, Judy."

Their father said nothing, but stared at Judy's little finger; and Daisy said: "The sugar went quick through the air. I saw it." But nobody paid any attention to Daisy, of course.

Judy began to say: "My little finger – "

But her mother interrupted her: "Judy, we don't want to hear any more at all about that little finger. There's nothing wrong with it."

So Judy said no more at all about her little finger; but it went on feeling very wrong.

Her father was the first to go, off to work. He kissed his wife goodbye, and his baby daughter, Daisy. He said, "Be a good boy!" to David, and he said, "Be a good girl!" to Judy. Then he stooped and kissed Judy, which he didn't usually do in the morning rush, and he whispered in her ear: "Watch out for that little finger of yours that wants to be crooked!"

Then he went off to work; and, a little later, Judy and David went off to school.

And Judy's little finger still felt wrong, aching and itching in its strange way.

Judy sat in her usual place in the classroom, listening to Mrs Potter reading a story aloud. While she listened, Judy looked round the classroom, and caught sight of an indiarubber she had often seen before and wished was hers. The indiarubber was shaped and coloured just like a perfect little pink pig with a roving eye. It belonged to a boy called Simon, whom she didn't know very well. Even if they had known each other very well indeed, he probably wouldn't have wanted to give Judy his perfect pink pig indiarubber.

As it was, Judy just stared at the indiarubber and longed to have it. While she longed, her little finger began to ache very much indeed and to itch very much indeed. It ached and itched to be allowed to crook itself, to beckon.

In the end Judy crooked her little finger.

Then there was a tiny sound like a puff of breath, and something came sailing through the air from Simon's table to Judy's table, and it landed with a little *flop!* just by Judy's hand. And Mrs Potter had stopped reading the story, and was crying: "Whatever are you doing, Simon Smith, to be throwing indiarubbers about? We don't throw indiarubbers about in this classroom!"

"I didn't throw my indiarubber!" said Simon. He was very much flustered.

"Then how does it happen to be here?" Mrs Potter had come over to Judy's table to pick up the indiarubber. She turned it over, and there was SIMON SMITH written in ink on the under side.

Simon said nothing; and, of course, Judy said nothing; and Mrs Potter said: "We *never* throw indiarubbers about in this classroom, Simon. I shall put this india-rubber up on my desk, and there it stays until the dinner-break."

But it didn't stay there – oh, no! Judy waited and waited until no one in the classroom – no one at all – was looking; and then she crooked her little finger, and the indiarubber came sailing through the air again – *flop!* on to her table, just beside her. This time Judy picked it up very quickly and quietly and put it into her pocket.

At the end of the morning, Simon went

up to Mrs Potter's desk to get his indiarubber back again; and it wasn't there. He
searched round about, and so did Mrs
Potter, but they couldn't find the indiarubber. In the end, Mrs Potter was both-
ered and cross, and Simon was crying.
They had no idea where the indiarubber
could have got to.

But Judy knew exactly where it was.

Now Judy knew what her little finger
could do – what it ached and itched to be
allowed to do. But she didn't want anyone
else to know what it could do. That would
have spoilt everything. She would have
had to return Simon's pink pig indiarubber
and anything else her little finger crooked
itself to get.

So she was very, very careful. At
dinner-time she managed to crook her little
finger at a second helping of syrup pudding, when no one was looking; and she
got it, and ate it. Later on, she crooked her
little finger at the prettiest seashell on the
Nature table, and no one saw it come
through the air to her; and she put it into
her pocket with the pink pig indiarubber.

Later still, she crooked her finger at another girl's hair-ribbon, that was hanging loose, and at a useful two-coloured pencil. By the end of the school day, the pocket with the pink pig indiarubber was crammed full of things which did not belong to Judy but which had come to her when she crooked her little finger.

And what did Judy feel like? Right in the middle of her – in her stomach – she felt a heaviness, because she had eaten too much syrup pudding.

In her head, at the very top of her head, there was a fizziness of airy excitement that made her feel almost giddy.

And somewhere between the top of her head and her stomach she felt uncomfortable. She wanted to think about all the things hidden in her pocket, and to enjoy the thought; but, on the other hand, she didn't want to think about them at all. Especially she didn't want to think about Simon Smith crying and crying for his pink pig indiarubber. The wanting to think and the *not* wanting to think made her feel very uncomfortable indeed.

When school was over, Judy went home with her brother, David, as usual. They were passing the sweetshop, not far from their home, when Judy said: "I'd like some chocolate, or some toffees."

"You haven't any money to buy chocolate or toffees," said David. "Nor have I. Come on, Judy."

Judy said: "Daisy once went in there, and the shopman gave her a toffee. She hadn't any money, and he *gave* her a toffee."

"That's because she was so little – a baby, really," said David. "He wouldn't give you a toffee, if you hadn't money to buy it."

"It's not fair," said Judy. And her little finger felt as if it agreed with her: it ached and it itched, and it longed to crook itself. But Judy wouldn't let it – yet. She and David passed the sweetshop and went on home to tea.

After tea, it grew dark outside. Indoors everyone was busy, except for Judy. Her mother was bathing Daisy and putting her to bed; her father was mending something; David was making an aeroplane out of numbered parts. Nobody was noticing Judy, so she slipped out of the house and went along the street to the sweetshop.

It was quite dark by now, except for the street-lamps. All the shops were shut; there was nobody about. Judy would have been frightened to be out alone, after dark, without anyone's knowing, but her little finger ached and her little finger itched, and she could think of nothing else.

She reached the sweetshop, and looked in through the window. There were pretty tins of toffee and chocolate boxes tied with bright ribbon on display in the window. She peered beyond them, to the back of the shop, where she could just see the bars of chocolate stacked like bricks and the rows of big jars of boiled sweets and the packets and cartons and tubes of sweets and toffees and chocolates and other delightful things that she could only guess at in the dimness of the inside of the shop.

And Judy crooked her little finger.

She held her little finger crooked, and she saw the bars of chocolate and the jars of boiled sweets and all the other things beginning to move from the back of the shop towards the front, towards the window. Soon the window was crowded close with sweets of all kinds pressing against the glass, as though they had come to stare at her and at her crooked little finger. Judy backed away from the shop window, to the other side of the street; but she still held her little finger crooked, and all the things in the sweetshop pressed up against the window, and pressed and crowded and pressed and pressed, harder and harder, against the glass of the shop window, until –

CRACK!

The window shattered, and everything in it came flying out towards Judy as she stood there with her little finger crooked.

She was so frightened that she turned and ran for home as fast as she could, and behind her she heard a hundred thousand things from the sweetshop come skittering and skidding and bumping and thumping along the pavement after her.

She ran and she ran and she reached her front gate and then her front door and she ran in through the front door and slammed it shut behind her, and heard all the things that had been chasing her come rattling and banging against the front door, and then fall to the ground.

Then she found that she had uncrooked her little finger.

Although she was safe now, Judy ran upstairs to her bedroom and flung herself upon her bed and cried. As she lay there, crying, she held her little finger out straight in front of her, and said to it: "I hate you – I HATE you!"

From her bed, she began to hear shouts and cries and the sound of running feet in the street outside, and her father's voice, and then her mother's, as they went out to see what had happened. There were people talking and talking, their voices high and loud with excitement and amazement. Later, there was the sound of a police car coming, and more talk.

127

But, in the end, the noise and the excitement died away, and at last everything was quiet. Then she heard footsteps on the stairs, and her bedroom door opened, and her father's voice said: "Are you there, Judy?"

"Yes."

He came in and sat down on her bed. He said that her mother was settling Daisy, so he had come to tell her what had been happening. He said there had been a smash-and-grab raid at the sweetshop. There must have been a whole gang of raiders, and they had got clean away: no one had seen them. But the gang had had to dump their loot in their hurry to escape. They had thrown it all – chocolates and toffees and sweets and everything – into the first convenient front garden. Judy's father said that the stuff had all been flung into their own front garden and against their own front door.

As she listened, Judy wept and wept. Her father did not ask her why she was crying; but at last he said: "How is that little finger?"

128

Judy said: "I hate it!"

"I daresay," said her father. "But does it ache and itch any more?"

Judy thought a moment. "No," she said, "it doesn't." She stopped crying.

"Judy," said her father, "if it ever starts aching and itching again, *don't crook it*."

"I won't," said Judy. "I never will again. Never. Ever."

The next day Judy went early to school, even before David. When she got into the classroom, only Mrs Potter was there, at the teacher's desk.

Judy went straight to the teacher's desk and brought out from her pocket the pink pig indiarubber and the shell and the hair-ribbon and the two-coloured pencil and all the other things. She put them on Mrs Potter's desk, and Mrs Potter looked at them, and said nothing.

Judy said: "I'm sorry. I'm really and truly sorry. And my father says to tell you that I had a crooked little finger yesterday. But it won't crook itself again, ever. I shan't let it."

"I've heard of crooked little fingers,"

said Mrs Potter. "In the circumstances, Judy, we'll say no more."

And Judy's little finger never crooked itself again, ever.

Acknowledgements

The editor and publishers gratefully acknowledge the following, for permission to reproduce copyright material in this anthology.

'The Thrush Girl' by Godfried Bomans, translated by Patricia Crompton, from *The Wily Wizard and the Wicked Witch* published by J. M. Dent 1969 copyright © Godfried Bomans, 1969 reprinted by permission of The Orion Publishing Group Ltd; 'The Tortoises' Picnic' by Katherine M. Briggs from *Folk Tales of England* published by Routledge and Kegan Paul 1965, copyright © Katherine M. Briggs, 1965, reprinted by permission of Routledge; 'How Trouble Made the Monkey Eat Pepper' by Grace Hallworth from *Listen to this Story* published by Methuen Children's Books 1977, copyright © Grace Hallworth, 1977, reprinted by permission of Reed Consumer Books; 'Anna-Magdalena's Dark Secret' by Kay Kinnear from *Anna-Magdalena Goes Head over Heels* published by Lion 1994, copyright © Kay Kinnear, 1994, reprinted by permission of Lion Publishing plc; 'Making Pancakes When My Mother was Out' and 'Ranjit and the Tiger' by Paddy Kinsale from *Bandwagon* published by Oxford University Press 1974, copyright © Paddy Kinsale, 1974, reprinted by permission of Barry Maybury; 'The Martian and the Supermarket', also known as 'Judy and the Martian', by

ACKNOWLEDGEMENTS

Penelope Lively, copyright © Penelope Lively, 1992, reprinted by permission of Macdonald Young Books, formerly Simon & Schuster Young Books; 'In the Beginning and Pandora's Box' by Geraldine McCaughrean from *The Orchard Book of Greek Myths* published by Orchard Books 1992, copyright © Geraldine McCaughrean, reprinted by permission of Orchard Books, 96 Leonard Street, London EC2A 4RH; 'The Crooked Little Finger' by Philippa Pearce from *Lion and School and Other Stories* published by Viking Kestrel 1985, copyright © Philippa Pearce, 1985, reprinted by permission of Penguin Books Ltd; 'The Leaning Silver Birch' by James Riordan from *Tales from Tartary* published by Kestrel Books 1978, copyright © James Riordan, 1978, reprinted by permission of Penguin Books Ltd; 'The Pearl Tree' by Ira Saxena, copyright © Ira Saxena, 1996, reprinted by permission of the author; 'Kind Polly and the Wolf in Danger' by Catherine Storr from *Last Stories of Polly and the Wolf* published by Faber and Faber 1990, copyright © Catherine Storr, 1990, reprinted by permission of Faber and Faber Ltd.

Thanks to Gay Elliott for 'Careless Conrad' by M. Joyce Davies, found in her wonderful collection of old books.

Puffin by Post

The Puffin Book of Stories for Six-Year-Olds

If you have enjoyed this book and want to read more,
then check out these other great Puffin titles.
You can order any of the following books direct with Puffin by Post:

Pirate School: Just a Bit of Wind • Jeremy Strong • 0141312696	£4.99
It's the first day at Pirate School with the fiercest headteacher in the universe! Perfect for developing readers.	

Pirate School: The Bun Gun • Jeremy Strong • 0141319267	£4.99
More hilarious adventures at the Pirate School. With brilliant colour illustrations throughout.	

The Witch's Dog and the Talking Picture • Frank Rodgers • 0141318147	£4.99
Magic and mayhem from Wilf and the witch's dog and his best friends. Gorgeous colour illustrations by the author throughout.	

The Robodog • Frank Rodgers • 0141310308	£4.99
How will Chip, the Robocop, get on with his new family? Find out in his first hilarious adventure.	

The Puffin Book of Stories for Seven-Year-Olds • Ed. Wendy Cooling • 0140374604	£4.99
The perfect story collection to share or read alone, for 'almost-sevens' and up!	

Just contact:

Puffin Books, C/o Bookpost, PO Box 29,
Douglas, Isle of Man, IM99 1BQ
Credit cards accepted. For further details:
Telephone: 01624 677237
Fax: 01624 670923

You can email your orders to: bookshop@enterprise.net
Or order online at: www.bookpost.co.uk

Free delivery in the UK.
Overseas customers must add £2 per book.

Prices and availability are subject to change.

Visit puffin.co.uk to find out about the latest titles, read extracts and
exclusive author interviews, and enter exciting competitions.
You can also browse thousands of Puffin books online.